TITCH
Dresses Up

Pat Hutchins

RED FOX

A Red Fox Book

Published by Random House Children's Books
20 Vauxhall Bridge Road, London SW1V 2SA

A division of Random House UK Ltd
London Melbourne Sydney Auckland
Johannesburg and agencies throughout the world

Copyright © Pat Hutchins 1998
Copyright © photographs Hutchins Film Company Limited

A Hutchins Film Company Limited production for Yorkshire Television

1 3 5 7 9 10 8 6 4 2

First published by Red Fox 1998

Printed and bound in Hong Kong.

RANDOM HOUSE UK Limited Reg. No. 954009

ISBN 0 09 926649 0

Titch was very excited.

His Mum had told him he could go to the fancy dress party with Peter and Mary. He wanted to go as a bird, but there wasn't much left in the dressing-up box.

Then Titch found a space helmet and decided to go as a spaceman. Although he really wanted to go as a bird.

'You're not going as a spaceman,' said Mary. 'I'm going as a spacewoman!'
 And she took the helmet.

So Titch looked in the box again.
    He found an Indian headdress, and decided to go as an Indian chief, although he really wanted to go as a bird.

'You're not going as an Indian chief!' said Peter.
'I am.'
    And Peter took the headdress.

So Titch looked in the box again. All that was left was a ragged cape.
  Maybe that would make him look like a bird!

'Do you think I look like a bird?'
he asked Peter.
　'No,' said
Peter.

So Titch went downstairs to ask Mum if she thought he looked like a bird.

Titch swooped around the
kitchen, and knocked a
colander onto his head.

'Do I look like a bird?' he asked Mum.
   'No,' she said. 'I think you look like a soldier.'

Titch wasn't sure he looked like a soldier, so he went to ask Dad what he thought.

'Do I look like a soldier?' Titch asked, though he really wanted to look like a bird.

'No,' said Dad. 'You look like Titch
with a colander on his head.'
    And Dad tied his handkerchief round
Titch's head. 'There!' he said. 'You can
go as a pirate!'

Titch wasn't sure he looked like a pirate, so he went upstairs to ask Mary what she thought.

'Do I look like a pirate?' asked Titch.

'No,' said Mary. 'You look like Titch with Dad's spotted handkerchief on your head. Why don't you go as a witch?'

And Mary put a witch's hat on his head.

But Titch wasn't sure he looked like a witch, so he went to ask Peter what he thought.

'Do I look like a witch?' he asked Peter.

'No,' said Peter, 'but you can go as an Indian chief. I've decided to go as a cowboy instead.'

And Peter put the headdress on Titch.

So Titch went to have a look at himself in the mirror. He still wasn't sure he looked like an Indian chief, and he really wanted to go to the party as a bird.

'Hurry up, Titch!' shouted Peter and Mary, 'We don't want to be late for the party!'
    So Titch hurried downstairs ...

...and stood on his chair to open the door.

Then. . . crash!

'Well,' said Mother and Father. 'That's not an Indian chief – it's a wonderful bird!'

'That's the best bird I've ever seen,' said Peter.

'I think Titch will have the best fancy dress at the party,' said Mary.

'I'm glad I'm a bird,' said Titch. 'I really wanted to go as a bird.'